Jim Hunter books

The Missing
Aircraft

Ben Butterworth and Bill Stockdale
Illustrated by Maureen and Gordon Gray

Fearon Education
a division of
David S. Lake Publishers
Belmont, California

Titles in the Series

United States edition published 1980 by David S. Lake Publishers,
19 Davis Drive, Belmont, California 94002. All rights reserved. No part
of this book may be reproduced by any means, transmitted or translated
into a machine language without written permission from the publisher.

First published 1977 by Methuen Educational
11 New Fetter Lane, London EC4P 4EE
Text © 1977 Ben Butterworth and Bill Stockdale
Illustrations © 1977 Maureen and Gordon Gray
Filmset in Photon Times 14 on 24 pt by
Richard Clay (The Chaucer Press) Ltd, Bungay, Suffolk
and printed in Great Britain by
Fletcher & Son Ltd, Norwich

ISBN-0-8224-3789-9

Printed in the United States of America

1. 9 8 7 6 5

The Missing Aircraft

'Have you ever been to Paranga?'

Colonel Johnson asked Jim Hunter.

'No,' replied Jim.

'It's a country in South America.

That's all I know about it.'

'I had an old friend in Paranga,'
said the Colonel,
'a chap called Harry Hammond.

He ran a small air cargo firm,
taking goods from Paranga
to the USA.
Now he has disappeared.

Jim, I want you to go to Paranga
and see if you can find him.

Domenico Branco - b - 19

Promoted general after Santos cou

I had better warn you too
that General Santos was the President
but he was shot dead a week ago.
The new President is General Branco.
He's a nasty bit of work
and so is his wife, Helen.
We think that Branco
had General Santos killed.'

no entry
einfahrt verboten

As soon as he landed
at Paranga airport
Jim could tell
he was being watched.
The customs men looked hard at him
and then at his passport.

It was dark

when Jim left the airport

and called a taxi.

'Hotel Madrid,' he told the driver.

As the taxi left the airport
by the main road
Jim saw a big black car
come up behind them.
'Do you speak English?'
Jim asked the driver.
'A little,' the driver said.
'My name is Pedro.'

'See the black car behind us?'
Jim said.
'When I shout, "Down,"
get down quickly.'

As the taxi left the main road
the black car pulled out to pass.
'Down,' shouted Jim.

Shots rang out from the black car
as it passed them, and bullets
whizzed over the front of the taxi.

'We live in bad times,' said Pedro.

'It was not like this

under General Santos.'

In the morning
Jim sent for Pedro again.

'Can you take me
to Hammond Airways?' he asked.

'Sure,' Pedro said.

'It's about a mile out of town.'

They stopped at a small airfield.

A girl was in the office.

'Could I have a word
with Mr. Hammond?' Jim asked.

'I'm afraid he's not here,'
said the girl.

'He took off for the USA ten days ago
with a new plane.

No one has seen him since.'

'What cargo was on the plane?'
Jim asked her.

'There was no cargo at all,'
the girl replied.

'General Santos just asked
Mr. Hammond to fly the new plane
to Washington for him.
It was just before the General died.'

Jim went back to the car.

'Now, Pedro,' he said.

'Why did the new plane disappear?

Why did Harry Hammond disappear?

Why did the plane have no cargo?'

'That's a lot of questions
for a poor man like me,' said Pedro.
'Tell me,' Jim went on,
'was General Santos a rich man?'
'No, no,' said Pedro.
'He died a poor man
in a poor country.
Branco soon found that out
after General Santos died.
All the country's gold has gone
and Branco can't last long
as President without that gold.'

When he got back to the hotel
Jim looked at a map of Paranga.
'Where could a plane come down?'
he said to himself.

Then he looked closer at the map.

'This part in the north

looks to me like desert,' he said.

Soon Pedro and Jim
were driving across the desert land.
They drove for miles,
but the land was empty.
There was nothing to be seen.
'Where on earth could a plane
land here?' asked Jim.

'Well,' Pedro said.
'I do seem to remember
an airstrip being made here in the war.
I think it's about five miles away.'
'Right, let's have a look,' said Jim.

They drove on
until they could see an old airstrip
with some huts nearby.
'Stop here, Pedro,' said Jim,
'and wait for me.'

He ran quickly

towards the nearest hut.

The big black car was outside.

Then – 'Hands up!'

Jim stopped
and put up his hands.

A tall young man
was waiting for him
on the roof of the hut.
His gun was pointing at Jim.

'Hi, Jim,' he said.

'What are you after?'

'Well, if it isn't Winston Power,'
Jim said.

'I'm after a man
called Harry Hammond.'

'That makes two of us,' said Winston,
'and two heads are better than one.'

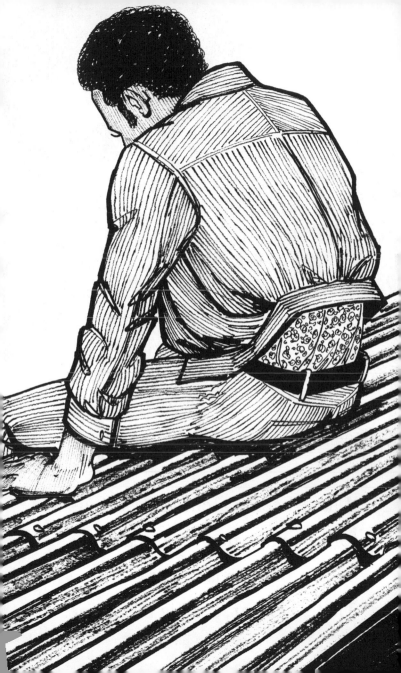

'I have been watching these huts
for two days now,' he went on.
'Helen Branco is inside.
That's her car, the big black one.'

'OK,' said Jim.

'Let's see what's going on in there.'

'Keep close to the huts,'

said Winston,

'and I will cover you from here.'

Jim ran from hut to hut

until he came to the biggest one.

Winston quickly followed him
and they peered into a tiny window.

Inside, parts of a small plane
were spread over the floor.
A man lay in a corner,
tied hand and foot.
A woman was talking
to three men in overalls.

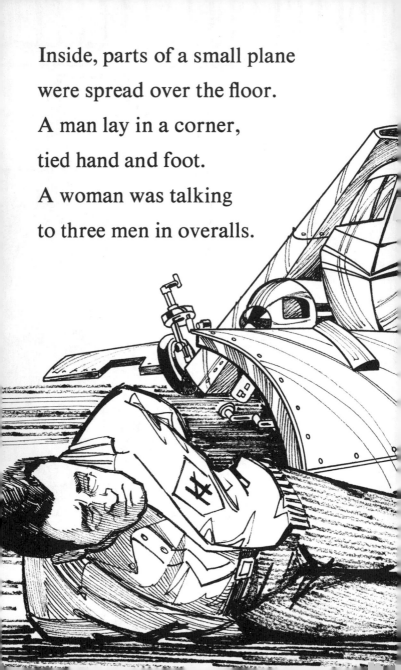

'It must be here,'

she was saying.

'It must be.'

She was stamping her foot in anger.

'That's Helen Branco,'

whispered Winston.

'We have taken this plane to bits,'
said one of the men,
'and I can tell you
there is no gold on it.'

'And this fool says he knows
nothing about it,' said Helen Branco,
waving her gun
at the man in the corner.
'For the last time, Hammond,
where is that gold?'

'Ready?' whispered Jim.

'Ready,' said Winston.

'You rush the door and
I will cover you from the window.'

As Jim smashed open the door
Winston fired two shots
over the heads of Helen Branco
and the three men.
'Drop that gun Helen,
and get over by the wall,' said Jim.
'Come on Winston,
tie this lot up,
and make sure of beautiful Helen.
She's behind all this.'

Jim went to the man on the floor
and cut him free.

'Harry Hammond?' he asked.

'That's me,' said the man.

'I'm Hunter, special agent, London,
and that's Power, CIA, Washington.
We were getting worried about you.'

'Tell me, Harry,' said Winston.

'How did you land up here?'

'That's easy,' said Harry.

'General Santos told Washington

that if Branco turned nasty

he would get the gold

out of his country, fast.

But Branco and his wife

hijacked the plane and

forced it down here.'

'They were sure
we were carrying the gold,
but I keep telling them
there was no cargo.'
'Did the plane fly well?' asked Jim.
'Not badly for a new plane,'
replied Harry Hammond,
'but it bumped a good deal
on take-off and landing.'

Jim looked at all the pieces
lying on the floor.
He picked up a knife
and scraped the paint
on one of the big wheels.
Under the paint
gold showed through.
'So that was the General's secret,'
said Winston in surprise.
'The plane had solid gold wheels.'

'What now?' asked Jim.

'Leave it to me,' said Winston.

'Washington has it all fixed

to take care of the gold.'

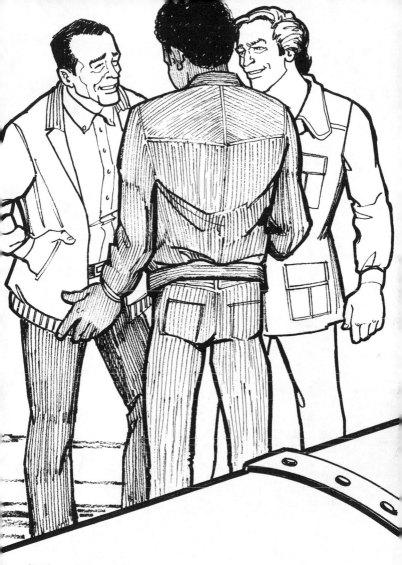

'Then I will take Harry
back to London with me,' said Jim.

'Colonel Johnson,' said Jim,

'I have an old friend to see you.'

'Harry!' said the Colonel.

'I'm glad to see you.'

'By the way, Colonel,' said Jim,
'here's a puzzle for you.

How do you fly gold out of Paranga
but not in a plane?'

'Not in a plane?' said the Colonel.
'I give up.'

'Don't worry,' said Jim.

'Harry will tell you the answer.'